AND THE BIG BAD WOLF

Who's afraid of the Big Bad Wolf? Chat show host Flash Eddie isn't. But more fool him!

Sam McBratney was a primary school teacher until becoming a full-time author. Twice winner of the Bisto Children's Book Award and once of a Bass Ireland Arts Prize, he has written many books, stories and radio plays for adults and children. His titles for Walker include *Art, You're Magic!*; *The Green Kids*; *In Crack Willow Wood*; *Oliver Sundew, Tooth Fairy* and the picture book *Guess How Much I Love You* (shortlisted for the Kurt Maschler Award and the British Book Awards: Illustrated Children's Book of the Year). He is married with three grown-up children and an elderly tortoise, and lives in County Antrim, Northern Ireland.

Books by the same author

Art, You're Magic!
The Green Kids
In Crack Willow Wood
Oliver Sundew, Tooth Fairy

FLASH EDDIE
☆ AND THE ☆
BIG BAD WOLF

SAM M^CBRATNEY

Illustrations by
HUNT EMERSON

WALKER BOOKS
AND SUBSIDIARIES
LONDON • BOSTON • SYDNEY

First published 1994 by Walker Books Ltd
87 Vauxhall Walk, London SE11 5HJ

This edition published 1995

2 4 6 8 10 9 7 5 3

This book has been typeset in Plantin.

Printed in England

British Library Cataloguing in Publication Data
A catalogue record for this book is available
from the British Library.

ISBN 0-7445-3696-0

Contents

Chapter One 7

Chapter Two 15

Chapter Three.......................................23

Chapter Four...31

Chapter Five..39

Chapter Six 49

Chapter Seven 61

Chapter Eight.......................................73

Chapter 1

Flash Eddie was going crazy. People had stopped watching his TV chat show and his boss was giving him a hard time.

"We're losing viewers, Eddie," she'd told him that very morning, "and viewers mean money. Isn't it about time you had someone interesting on your show for a change?"

As if interesting people fell out of the blue sky! Eddie put his face in his hands to shut out this cruel world and wondered if maybe the Queen or the Pope would come on the show. Or even a giant panda. People loved pandas, they were so cuddly and cute.

His assistant, who was called Sadie Tuffett, poked him in the arm. "There's a letter here from a man who says he's got a boxing guinea-pig. It wears teeny little boxing gloves on its front paws."

"Gimme a break," said Eddie. "What about the Palace? Any word from the Palace?"

"Just a letter saying that the Royals never give interviews on chat shows."

"Snobs," Eddie muttered rather desperately as he glanced at the list in his hand. The winner of the last big snooker tournament was willing to come on the show. And the author of a book about oyster-farming... Yet another Oscar-winning movie star... A pop singer... A walnut-juggling parrot... Stone me, thought Eddie, they'll put the audience to sleep in five minutes flat.

"Where are all the interesting people, anyway?" he cried. "Are they extinct? We need somebody glamorous, rich, intelligent, witty, exciting. If only I could interview myself!" He hammered a fist into his palm. "Come on, Eddie, think big! What about China?"

"China?" enquired Sadie.

"Yeah, China. We've had half of America on this show but nobody from China, which has more people than any other country in the world. There must be somebody interesting in China." A loud knock interrupted Eddie in full flight. "Get that blasted door."

"Yes, Master."

"And I'm not in, right? I'm busy. Tell whoever it is to come back in ten years."

What about Bobby Charlton, thought Eddie? But I'd need a new angle, they've all seen him before...

He got up and stood in front of the mirror – the place where he rehearsed all his interviews.

"Ladies and gentlemen," he said quietly, "I will now ask Bobby Charlton to take off his socks and shoes. These are the actual feet that scored forty-nine goals for England. Folks, forget about 1066. I ask you to remember 1966 – would we have won the World Cup without the feet you see before you now...?"

Sadie came in and interrupted this performance with a little cough. She didn't seem put out by the sight of her superior in bare feet and with his trouser leg rolled up.

"I don't know which are more dazzling, Eddie – the rings on your fingers, the ties round your neck or the socks you wear."

"Mind your manners, Sunshine, and get me some coffee."

"I got you coffee five minutes ago, my name isn't Sunshine and the guy at the door says he used to be the Big Bad Wolf."

"Yeah, and I used to be Donald Duck. Tell him..." Eddie paused. "He used to be what?"

Slow down a minute here, thought Eddie, this might be interesting. Probably a nutcase, of course, but these were desperate times...

"I told him you were busy," said Sadie, "but he just looked at me and whispered, 'Time is not one of my problems.' He gives me the creeps."

"Really?" Who knows, maybe I won't have to go to China after all, thought Eddie. "Wheel him in, Sunshine."

To say that the Wolf walked into Eddie's office would be an exaggeration, for he hobbled in on a walking-stick. His head was bald, his ears drooped and his tail looked like a bit of chewed rope. Stone me, thought

Eddie, he's escaped from the pantomime! He had one last lonely tooth in his lower jaw. His eyes were dark and deep, though – something about them sent a shiver up Eddie's spine.

All the better to see you with, my dear.

"Sit down, Wolfy, you look like you could use a chair!"

"Thank you kindly," came the soft reply. Something creaked as the visitor sat down. Maybe it was the chair, maybe it was the Wolf. Should I offer him a drink or a cigar, Eddie wondered. Merciful heaven, was this really the awful creature of legend sitting in his office as large as life? No, it couldn't be.

Could it?

Chapter 2

"Flash Eddie is my name, sir, TV is my game. And this is my assistant producer, Miss Sadie Tuffett. You're very welcome."

The Wolf offered to shake Sadie's hand, but she clearly felt that she might not get it back, and retreated two steps.

"And how about yourself, sir," Eddie went on. "What do your friends call you?"

"Friends?" A sad and virtually toothless smile appeared on the face of the Wolf. "I'm afraid that I have always been something of a lone wolf, so to speak. The few friends I did have never seemed to last."

"Why was that, Wolfy?"

"I ate them."

Without saying a word, Eddie crossed the room to whisper in the small pink ear of his assistant.

"Did you hear what I just heard?"

"Of course I heard! Get rid of him now, Eddie."

"He ate his best friends. Is this guy for real?"

"I wouldn't trust him as far as I could throw

him. Look, he knows we're talking about him!"

The Wolf had produced a newspaper cutting, which he now presented for their inspection.

"I am here because of your advert. It says: *Guests wanted for our nation's favourite TV chat show. Do not apply if you are dull or boring.* Perhaps it's a silly thought, but I wondered if you might like to have me on your show. I *have* been something of a celebrity in my time."

Eddie whipped off his shades in time to see Sadie jerking her thumb towards the door. That thumb meant "Do Bobby Charlton, Eddie, go to China if you must." But if this joker turned out to be who he said he was, every viewer in the land would be stuck to their seats in front of the telly. Without glue.

"Let's get this straight, Wolfy – you're the one who almost got Little Red Riding Hood, right? You are *that* wolf?"

"I am he."

Sadie spoke up. She couldn't help it. "He actually admits it! Don't you think it's a little wrong to go round eating people?"

"I'm sure you're right," the Wolf replied gently, "but I do find it difficult to live on vegetable soup. In any case, the little girl got away. My disguise let me down, I think."

"You were disguised as her granny," cried Sadie. "Whom you had just eaten, you beast!"

"Believe me, I can understand your feelings very well," said the Wolf, apparently unmoved by this outburst. "But in our youth we all do things that we might not do when we're older and wiser."

"Huh, that's rich! Any goofball can say he's sorry, but being sorry doesn't change anything, does it? Being sorry doesn't butter any parsnips!"

The Wolf seemed quietly puzzled. "I didn't actually say that I was sorry, and I'm afraid I've never had much to do with parsnips."

Eddie brought his hands together with a

clap. There were more important things to talk about than parsnips. What a break, he was thinking! *Big Bad Wolf, This Is Your Life.* Oh, man.

"OK, Wolfy, I'm thinking of putting you on the show and I'm going to talk this over with my boss. Don't you run away now, you hear? And if you want a drink of water or anything, just ask Sadie."

With those words, Eddie whizzed through a door labelled JOYCE FIZZ. Sadie, abandoned, couldn't help noticing how the Wolf's nose twitched when he looked at her out of those yellow eyes. Once, he even moistened his lips with that disgusting, lollopy, big, pink tongue. Then he noticed the tank of fish in the corner.

"Ah. I see you've got goldfish," he said, presumably to make polite conversation. "They are very restful to watch, I'm told. I myself have always been fond of ornamental carp."

"There are seven of them," snapped Sadie,

just to let him know they'd been counted.

She wasn't in the mood for polite conversation, and decided that now was a good time to go and post some letters. The Wolf rose to open the door for her, saying, "Allow me."

"No, I don't allow you," came the reply. "I can open my own doors, thanks very much."

Chapter 3

Flash Eddie's boss gazed through a window to where the Wolf sat in a chair nursing his walking-stick and staring at the goldfish.

Joyce Fizz was a tough lady. She had been in the TV business for a long time. She knew that some folks would pull any kind of trick to get their faces on the box. Experience had made her careful and suspicious. And if that was the Big Bad Wolf in there, he didn't look very big or terribly bad.

"There's more life in a hearthrug, Eddie," she pointed out.

"Well, he's past his sell-by date," said Eddie.

"There are two questions I want to put to you," said Joyce, "and the first one is this: are you sure it's him?"

"It's him all right," said Eddie. "He's got a kind of presence about him. I mean, he didn't rush in saying, 'I'm the Big Bad Wolf and I'm famous and you'd better put me on your show or I'll bite your head off, gnash-gnash-gnash.'" Eddie snapped at the air three times for effect. "No. He talks quietly. He knows who he is. He's confident. Yeah. He's the real thing."

But Joyce Fizz glanced through the window once again. That walking-stick... And the tail looked as though it had been made by someone learning to knit.

"I expected something a little more menacing. Dangerous, even."

"He's an old-age pensioner, for crying out loud," cried Eddie. "Look, let's face it, we all lose a bit of the old fire in the belly when the end's in sight, right? Come on, JF, what's your second question?"

"OK, let's assume that he's the genuine article. The next question is – would the viewers find him interesting?"

"Are you kidding? He can't miss!"

"Convince me," said Joyce Fizz.

Eddie grabbed a thick phone book and held it under his boss's chin. And when he spoke, he spoke with some passion. "Here – find me just one name in this book of a

thousand pages who hasn't heard of the
Big Bad Wolf. They'll love him! JF, we can't
lose – this is one of the all-time-great bad
guys in the history of the human race out
there. And people just love to hate a bad guy!
They'll write letters, they'll make phone calls,
they'll want the show banned, the publicity
will be unbelievable. Everybody will say,
'How shocking this is!' and they'll all watch
every second because you know why? They
want to be shocked, that's why!"

"And what will you talk to him about on
the show?" asked Joyce Fizz after a pause.

Gimme a break, thought Eddie, he's only
just walked in the door.

"I don't know, the usual stuff... His
childhood, Mum, Dad, brothers and sisters,
his hobbies. I'll ask him to describe some of
the bad things he's done in life."

"Ours is a family show, Eddie, it goes out
early in the evening."

"But I'll get him to say he's sorry!" Eddie
began to move about the room, shaping his

interview. It was as if he was now actually talking to the Wolf in front of millions of viewers all holding their breath. "And if you had your time again, Wolfy, what would you change? Would you do those things again, or would you be a different and a better kind of wolf?" He swung round to face his boss, excitement in his voice. "Wouldn't it be just wonderful if he broke down and cried? Tears are beautiful on TV."

Just for a moment, Joyce Fizz seemed impressed. A hint of a smile tugged at the lips which she kept shining red for a large part of the day.

"All right, we'll go for it. Talk to him some more and find out if he's a fake. And Eddie" – the smile was gone – "you'd better be sure about this one. You know how many people watched your show in May? Eight million. In July it was six million. By August it was down to three million. We're losing viewers, Eddie."

"Everybody's away in August," Eddie

pointed out, "the country's empty. They're all in Crete or Cyprus."

"That's as may be, but if things don't change there'll be nobody watching your show by Christmas and I don't have to remind you that viewers mean money. There are big companies out there trying to sell cars and baked beans and soap – they're not going to advertise on FIZZ TV if there's nobody watching us. So please get it right or people are going to be asking for your head on a plate."

And you're the very girl to give it to them, thought Eddie as he returned to his office.

Chapter 4

When Eddie walked back into his office, the Wolf looked up and smiled. What a big mouth you have, thought Eddie.

Then he saw that Sadie wasn't in her chair. Or even in the room!

Or was she? A horrible thought loomed up in Eddie's mind. Surely she hadn't been... Somehow he couldn't bring himself to finish the sentence.

Calm down, Eddie, don't be so stupid! Sure enough, at that moment Sadie breezed through the door as large as life. She looked at Eddie, looked at the Wolf, looked at the goldfish, and sat down at her computer. Eddie was about to ask her for coffee when he saw the words appearing on the screen: I AM AN ASSISTANT PRODUCER, NOT THE TEA GIRL. GET IT YOURSELF, SUNSHINE. AND GET RID OF YOU-KNOW-WHO.

I must give that girl a good talking-to, thought Eddie, or else buy her some perfume. But right now he had other things on his mind.

"OK, Wolfy, you're on the show. I talked things over with my boss and she says you can have one hundred pounds appearance money. How does that grab you?"

"Thank you," said the Big Bad Wolf ever so quietly, "although I must point out that a hundred pounds will not buy many pork chops at today's prices."

"Beast!" cried Sadie.

"Take it or leave it, old son," said Eddie.

"Oh, I'll take it," said the Wolf.

Sadie spun round in her office swivel chair. "Talking of pork chops, what about the Three Little Pigs – remember them? Didn't you fall down their chimney into a pot of boiling water and that was the end of you? How do you explain that?"

With an air of great patience, the Wolf leaned forward and settled the point of his chinny-chin-chin on the handle of his stick.

"The story is wrong, I'm afraid. I'm very much alive. No sensible person would climb down a chimney with smoke and steam coming out of it. You see, to be sure of a happy ending the writers of stories often make up things which never happened."

"But you did try and blow their house down, didn't you?" snapped Sadie. "All that huffing and puffing wasn't just bluffing."

"Well, yes, I admit that I did try a trick or two to scare them into surrendering."

"Huh!" muttered Sadie.

Eddie decided that it was time to end this nonsense. He draped a friendly arm around the Wolf's neck.

"Let's not beat about the bush, Wolfy. If you're going to be on the show we'll have to know all about you. What were you like when you were an itty-bitty baby? That'd be the stuff the viewers go for. Make 'em laugh and make 'em cry, that's what I always say. You weren't an orphan by any chance?"

"No."

"Pity, it helps if they feel sorry for you. What were you like as a youngster? I bet you were the toughest kid on the block."

The chair creaked again – or maybe it was Wolfy's bones – as the visitor struggled to an upright position.

"Not at all, I was very shy and often ran away from foxes who called me names. But I think I must go home now. One gets tired so easily these days. Many years ago a woodcutter struck me on the right hip with his axe, and he left me with a weakness there which has become worse in recent years."

"You poor thing," growled Sadie. The Wolf ignored her.

"Do you think we could talk some more tomorrow? We could meet in the park at the edge of town. Would that be convenient? How about three o'clock in the afternoon?"

"You and me at three, Wolfy," said Flash Eddie.

"Then … goodbye."

Eddie was happy. For a time he buzzed about the office talking about how he was going to make television history. He even made coffee for Sadie.

"Oh man, I stand on the brink of everlasting Greatness! *Flash Eddie meets the Big Bad Wolf.* For the first time ever on the small screen, folks, The Beast Who Gave You Nightmares. Right there in your living-room! Oh, lucky day, they'll talk about this for years. You want some sugar, Sunshine?"

"No," said Sunshine, as she tapped on the glass front of the fish tank with a pencil.

"What's up with the fish?" asked Eddie.

"I'm counting them, Eddie, that's what's up with the fish. There are still seven."

Eddie stirred in his own sugar madly. "Well, whaddyaknow, poor old Wolfy was a shy kid. Who'd have thought it?"

Shy my eye, thought Sadie. Another word came to her mind that rhymed with shy.

Sly.

Chapter 5

Flash Eddie, Sadie and the Big Bad Wolf circumnavigated the lake in the park.

They circumnavigated slowly, of course, for Wolfy wasn't the fastest thing ever seen on a walking-stick. The old boy's jogging days are over, Eddie thought with a smile.

"You all right, Wolfy? You only have to say the word, pal, and we'll take it easy."

"Not at all. The exercise will do me good, I'm sure."

Sadie, who had been very quiet, suddenly spoke up. "There aren't any ducks!"

"Ducks?" enquired Eddie.

"There's something strange about this place today. There aren't any ducks. There should be ducks."

True enough, thought Eddie. Normally you couldn't move one foot past the other without tripping over the blasted quackers.

"Bread is no good for them any more, you know," he said, to make polite conversation. "The modern duck expects you to feed him *cake*! Do you like ducks, Wolfy?"

"Very much so," came the reply. "Ducks have a strong dark taste which is pleasantly oily, and far superior to chicken. Still, even a chicken a day can keep hunger at bay." And here the Wolf paused to smile a sad little smile. "If only one had the teeth for it, of course."

"That's not what he meant," snapped Sadie. "He didn't mean do you like to *eat* ducks."

"Now, now," said Eddie, "let's not get all worked up. Everybody eats turkeys and chickens. We're all carnivores, here – right? Let's sit down over there and take the weight off our legs."

They sat down on a bench between the water and a grandly weeping willow. Lovely spot, thought Eddie, perfect for an outside broadcast: *Flash Eddie meets the Big Bad Wolf in the park*. Good idea. Very natural.

"OK, let's get on with this. Sunshine here can take notes while you tell us a bit about yourself, Wolfy. What were you like at school, for instance? You did go to school, I take it?"

"Yes indeed, I went to school. I'm afraid I didn't do very well there."

"No brains, huh?"

"Oh, I think I was intelligent enough," said the Wolf, "but they made me leave all the same."

"Come on, Wolfy, spill the beans."

The Wolf stroked the last few hairs on his chinny-chin-chin. "There was a little misunderstanding about school dinners. To cut a long story short, I ate my teacher."

"You ate your teacher?" cried Sadie, jumping to her feet. "And you call that 'a little misunderstanding'? You barbarian! You can't go round eating teachers as if they were on the *menu*!"

This last word from Sadie was delivered with a shriek.

"You're being hostile, Sunshine," Eddie pointed out.

"I *feel* hostile. He's a total savage!"

"It's quite all right, I assure you," said the

Wolf. "I often arouse strong feelings in people."

"I'll bet!" cried Sadie, as she threw the Biro she had been taking notes with into the lake.

At this point Eddie got up and steered her away by the elbow.

"Now listen here, my little assistant producer," he whispered confidentially. "Most of the people we interview are jerks, right? If we only interviewed the people we like there might be a show every ten years if we got lucky. OK, so Wolfy here wouldn't be one hundred per cent welcome at the teddy bears' picnic, but that's no reason for us to be unprofessional. This here ain't no poodle, you know. He's a Wolf!"

Having made his point, Eddie turned and smiled the kind of smile which smooths things over. "No offence meant, Wolfy old son."

"None taken, I assure you," said the Wolf.

"And was that the end of your schooldays, then?"

"I tried to stay on," continued the Wolf, "but the Head Teacher would not listen to me. He had made up his mind that I must go, and would not give me a second chance."

"A second *helping*, you mean!" yelled Sadie.

Eddie imagined the scene – the Head pointing with a big long arm towards the gate, Wolfy down on his knees, begging to stay on and do his reading. Maybe the Head was still alive. Get him on the programme too! Oh, lucky day.

Using his stick, the Wolf prised himself off the bench. "Could I just ask you, Eddie... You don't mind if I call you Eddie?"

"Be my guest, Wolfy!"

"Thank you. Could I just ask you to tell me a little more about your plans for the show? After all, television can be a stressful experience for those of us who are not used to the cameras."

"Sure," said Eddie, "what do you want to know?"

"Oh... How long will the interview last, and seating arrangements, and, well, many things. But I think that perhaps I've had enough for today. Do you think we could meet tomorrow at the edge of the woods? I find it extremely tiring to come all the way into town, and I haven't been eating too well recently."

"You poor little thing," muttered Sadie.

"No problem," said Eddie. "And Sunshine here will bring along your appearance money."

"Sunshine will do no such thing," said Sadie. "I won't be there. You can take your own notes."

Suit yourself, thought Eddie as he turned to put Wolfy at his ease. "Don't be worrying about any of this, pal, we're going to have ourselves the show of the century. Here's what I'm going to do. Tonight, I'll jot down a few questions for you to have a look at. How does that grab you?"

"Thank you. Naturally I'll do what I can to

answer them as fully and as truthfully as possible."

Eddie laughed. The truth didn't bother him – it only made people think. He believed in telling the viewers anything so long as it made them feel good. Make the zombies laugh, make 'em cry, make 'em watch the next show – that was Flash Eddie's style.

"Until tomorrow, then, at the edge of the woods," said the Wolf with a faint smile; then he was gone.

And when the Wolf had gone, the strangest thing happened. All the ducks came back and the air was filled with happy quacks.

Funny about the ducks, thought Eddie.

Chapter 6

That night, Flash Eddie sat in front of his word-processor. He was making pretty good progress with his script. The screen said:

TEN QUESTIONS FOR OLD WOLFY

1   What's your hobby?

2   What's your favourite pop group?

3   Any advice for kids today?

4   Name your all-time-great movie star.

5   What makes you laugh?

6   What's the world's greatest invention?

7   What makes you cry?

8   Are you truly sorry for anything you've done?

9   Any personal problems?

Only nine questions. He needed one more. Think of the viewers, Eddie – what do they like to hear…?

Got it! Eddie typed in his last question (When did you have your first kiss?) and went off to bed.

The woods were gloomy, dark and deep when

Flash Eddie arrived there the following evening. The sun was setting rather beautifully, but Eddie hardly noticed it. He didn't really like the countryside. It was too quiet. Not enough action! The country was all very well for pretty buttercups and daisies and things with roots, but it wasn't for a fast mover like Eddie who'd never owned a pair of wellies in his life.

Looking round, he wondered about the birds. Not a thrush or a blackbird or a robin in sight. Weren't the cheepers supposed to sing their heads off in these pastures green? Funny about the birds.

Then he saw the Wolf watching him from under a big tree.

"Wolfy! Nice to see you, pal, how's the old leg, then?"

"A touch of arthritis, I'm afraid."

"Oh well, none of us lives for ever – right? Got your money here, one hundred lovely smackers. There you go, that'll keep the wolf from the door."

The Wolf accepted the money with a smile. "I'm most grateful."

"Don't mention it. I've also got some questions for you; you know, the sort of thing we might talk about on the show. What are your hobbies, for instance?"

"My hobbies?"

"Yeah. Do you go in for hang-gliding or knitting, or what?"

"Well... I like to make up poems, and say them to myself as I wander through the woods on warm summer evenings."

Stone me, he's a poet! Must get him to say one or two on the show. Be a laugh. Eddie wrote POET on his clipboard, saying, "You've had a busy life, Wolfy – have you any advice for kids growing up in today's world?"

"Yes indeed. Stay away from geese."

"Stay away from geese?"

"A goose gave me a black eye long ago," said the Wolf, "and it's something I've never forgotten."

STAY AWAY FROM GEESE wrote Eddie. Oh

man, that is priceless! "Right! In your opinion, what is the world's greatest invention?"

A pause. Then: "I would say toothpaste."

Jeepers. Toothpaste! "OK, let's move on to music. What's your favourite group?"

"The London Philharmonic Orchestra."

Heavy, heavy! "Personal problems now, Sunshine. What's your biggest personal problem?"

"What sort of personal problems?"

"Any sort – do you miss your mum, do you have bad dreams, do you come out in spots...?"

"I get the occasional flea."

THE FLEAS THAT TEASE... wrote Eddie, swatting a fly away from his nose. It was a little darker, now. A thin moon, turned up at the ends, glowed in the sky and reminded him of a grinning mouth in a Hallowe'en turnip.

"Suppose you weren't a wolf, Wolfy – what would you like to be?"

"A whale."

"You'd like to be a whale?"

"Only if I had to stop being a wolf."

"We'll skip that one," said Eddie, who was confused. "What's the hardest thing you've ever had to do in your life?"

"Eat a tortoise. Have you ever tried to eat a tortoise?"

"Not recently, Wolfy, no."

"It's all shell, top and bottom. I honestly believe that they are worse than hedgehogs to get at. Most inconvenient."

Unless you're the tortoise, thought Eddie, settling a friendly arm around the shoulder of the Wolf and leading him out from the trees to stand under the clear evening sky. A big moment was coming up.

"Look out there, Wolfy. What do you see? You see the lights of a city sparkling in the distance under a fingernail moon. The moon is turned up at the ends – you see? It's glowing, rather like the mouth of a turnip glows at Hallowe'en."

"I've never had much to do with turnips," said the Wolf.

"Never mind that now. The heat has gone out of the day, it's getting dark and there's only you and me. On the night of the show I'm going to turn to you and I'm going to say in a low voice – 'And what about regrets, Wolfy? Would you like to say a big SORRY if you had the chance?' And Wolfy…"

"Yes?"

"That's when I want you to imagine that there's only you and me, like there is tonight. And I want you to tell it from here!"

And so saying, Eddie beat slowly on his heart with a closed fist. He wished that the old boy would hurry up and answer. Maybe Wolfy was sorry about everything. Maybe he would break down on the show and cry his eyes out. The viewers would love it.

"Yes, I suppose there is one thing I regret," said the Wolf. "One day – I remember that it was very windy – a strange creature came running through the woods. It was round and brightly coloured, with spikes sticking out of it. Probably I wouldn't have chased it if it hadn't run away from me." The Wolf shook his head sadly. "Of course I was young then, and hadn't much experience of the world. I'd never seen an umbrella before, and so I tried to eat it."

Silly big twit, thought Eddie. Nice story, though. The viewers liked a laugh.

"You regret eating the umbrella?"

"Not exactly. I broke my tooth on it, you see, and went to the dentist. Unfortunately I hadn't eaten a thing for two or three days."

"And so?"

"Well, I was very, very hungry."

The penny dropped. Actually, it felt more like a pound coin. Oh, stone me, thought Eddie.

"You didn't eat your dentist!"

The Wolf pushed himself away from the branch that was propping him up and leaned on his stick.

"But I don't want to keep you talking all

night," he said wearily. "After all, these events happened so very long ago… I have been doing some thinking about your show. Why don't you come and film it in my home? It's just through there, in the heart of the woods. I'm sure that your viewers would find it most interesting."

Super idea, thought Eddie. True to life. Lots of mood. *Flash Eddie talks to the Big Bad Wolf in his den.*

"You wouldn't mind the cameras?" he said.

"Not at all. Perhaps you could come along tomorrow and see for yourself whether it is suitable for all your equipment? Your assistant is welcome too, of course."

"You make her nervous, Wolfy, but I'll be there."

"Then shall we say … about lunchtime?"

"It's a date!" said Eddie.

"Excellent." Two moist eyes flashed with moonlight; then the Wolf was gone.

On the way back to his sports car with the black and gold trim, Eddie rubbed his hands with delight. Sheer glee bubbled up inside him as he paused for a moment to talk to an imaginary audience of many millions: "Ladies and gentlemen, he calls himself a poet. This monster ate his teacher, he ate his dentist, he even eats umbrellas. In his youth he was beaten up by a goose, he likes the London Philharmonic and he's got fleas. Who am I talking about? I am talking about your guest for this evening! Into your living-room tonight Flash Eddie brings ... the Big Bad Wolf."

And then a strange thing happened. Just as Eddie reached his car some little birds began to sing their songs from the woods' dark fringe.

Funny about the birds, thought Eddie.

Chapter 7

It rained out of the heavens all night.

By the time Flash Eddie made it to the woods next day, the path to old Wolfy's place glistened with puddles. And all you could hear was the hollow echo of trees dripping after rain.

Luckily he had his golfing umbrella. Better not let go of it or Wolfy will have it for lunch, Eddie thought with a grin.

Umbrella for lunch! You had to admit it was funny.

What was happening to his lovely leather Italian shoes wasn't funny, though. The poor things looked like blobs of mud. But when Eddie came into a clearing and saw the Wolf's den, he forgot about his shoes.

Magic! Five rusty pillars (four oil drums and an ex-bath) held up the roof, where a fine crop of dandelions waved their yellow heads. The chimney pot was a tin of Quality Street, and plastic windows flapped in the walls. Stone me, thought Eddie. What a dump! The viewers would love it.

A voice said "Come in" when he rapped on the door, so in he went.

"Wolfy, Wolfy, Wolfy, what a day! Look what the puddles have done to my shoes. Man, this is the back of beyond."

The Wolf, in a striped butcher's apron, smiled, and said, "I'm so pleased you could make it."

"It takes more than a few drops of rain to keep Flash Eddie away from a good story."

"But don't you have wellington boots?"

"Ha!" cried Eddie. "Wolfy, here's a tip – if you want to get ahead in TV, stay out of welly boots. Bad for the old image." And he shook hands with the Wolf most sincerely. "How you bin, pal?"

"Fine. Yes, I've been fine. Let me take your umbrella."

"Don't eat it, Wolfy! I need that umbrella for golf. So this is where it all happens, eh? Wolfy's den! I couldn't help noticing your chimney on the way in. It looks like a sweetie tin."

"With the bottom knocked out of it, of course," smiled the Wolf. "When one lives so far from civilization, one has to make do."

Hmm, thought Eddie, looking out of a window. And one certainly does live far from civilization. Funny thing, he hadn't seen a sign of a single animal on the way here. Was the forest empty?

"Not much life around here, Wolfy. 'Course I'm only a towny, never owned a pair of wellies in my life, but I thought that lots of furry little animals lived in the woods. Stoats and badgers and little bunny rabbits, stuff like that."

"Not round here," said the Wolf. "They tend to stay away."

"No neighbours, huh?"

"Neighbours?" the Wolf said softly. "Neighbours are like friends – I don't seem to be able to keep them very long."

Something in that voice made Eddie pause momentarily; then he stared in amazement as the Wolf cast off his apron. The old fleabag was all dressed up. In a suit! The suit had seen better days, of course, but then so had everything else in this joint.

"Say, Wolfy, you look like a million dollars. And this is some place you've got here!"

"Thank you. I like to think of a meal as something of an occasion."

"You should have told me, pal, I'd have smartened myself up a bit."

"Not at all. I would say – " and here the Wolf paused before he finished – "I would say that you have excellent ... taste."

"Taste?" said Eddie.

"By 'taste' I mean your sense of style."

"Yeah, well, I've always had style," Eddie agreed. "It's a thing you're born with, Wolfy – you've either got it or you haven't. They can't teach you style in school and you can't buy it. It's just there."

"Quite."

Now the Wolf began to lay some utensils on the table. The glory days are over for him, thought Eddie. No more teachers and dentists. Probably the old boy dips his crusts in his tea. Where to put the cameras in this shack, that was the problem. One by the door, perhaps, and one in the corner to take in the fireplace. Keep everything cosy, that was the secret and the magic of TV. Make the paying customers think they're right in there where the action is. Millions of them!

"There's a TV in every home, Wolfy – did you ever think of that? The cameras are at the football match and the boxing ring and the Houses of Parliament and there's hardly a monkey in the jungle that hasn't starred in some nature programme. I tell you, the sun never sets in this business."

"You don't think of it as a kind of monster?" said the Wolf as he sharpened a knife.

"TV? A monster? Listen, pal, I'd be selling used cars on the Old Kent Road if it wasn't for TV."

"But don't some people say that television is already beyond our control? Every day it presents us with powerful images that we can't cope with. We don't even know yet that we can't cope with them."

"Only if you watch the News, Wolfy. The News would put anybody off their dinner. Look, people watch TV for one reason only – to escape from the hole they're living in. It's like a big adventure machine with a big slot that you can put your whole self into."

"I'm sure you're right, Eddie," said the Wolf.

You bet I'm right, thought Eddie, who suddenly had a great idea. A wind machine! On the night of the interview there could be a gale howling in the background. Great touch! Attention to detail – you couldn't beat it.

Then he noticed the walking-stick hanging on the back of the door. Funny, the old boy looked quite light on his feet today. Must have had a couple of pep pills.

"I'll just lock the door," said the Wolf, passing him by to put a key in the lock. "Sometimes it blows open."

"But it's not windy."

"One never knows," the Wolf said softly.

Without quite knowing why, Eddie began to feel just a little bit uncomfortable as he watched the Wolf preparing the table for lunch. What was on the menu, he couldn't help wondering? By chance their eyes met, the Wolf smiled, and Eddie gave a little shiver as he glanced at the locked door.

Home time, he decided. "Well, Wolfy, I must go, no need to hang about, as they say. Your place is fine, let me tell you, just fine. It'll do just great for the show."

"But we haven't had lunch," said the Wolf.

"I had a late breakfast, Wolfy. And now I must get back to work – no rest for the wicked, ha!"

As Eddie reached for his umbrella, the Wolf reached for a jar on a high shelf. This jar he set down in the middle of the table.

"Tell me, Eddie, have you ever heard people talking about a thing called 'the quality of life'?"

"The quality of life?" Jeepers, what was this all about? "Yeah, sure, the quality of life. What about it?"

"Well, I never knew what those words meant until I had these made for me." The Wolf tapped the jar in the middle of the table. "They have certainly improved my quality of life."

Eddie mopped his brow with a gaudy hanky. Oh, stone me! All of a sudden the Wolf was wearing two rows of teeth, top and bottom.

He's got false teeth!

"I only wear them indoors," the Wolf explained ever so quietly. "For eating. They're as sharp as icicles, I find. And do you know, I believe they're even better than the real thing. Sucking soup through a straw is all very well – but meat is meat. What do you think?"

Eddie swallowed once and he swallowed twice. Right now he didn't know whether he felt too hot or too cold. He sure didn't feel normal.

"I mean, what do you think of my teeth? All the better to eat with, wouldn't you say?"

Eddie tried to tell a joke he knew about false teeth, but the words got stuck in his throat as the Wolf flashed him an awesome smile. There was nothing funny about that mouthful of gnashers. Oh, man!

"Kinda warm in here, don't you think, Wolfy? You couldn't open a window or something?"

"Let's not think about windows," came the reply. "Let's think of something much more interesting than windows. Let's think about lunch."

"Lunch?" croaked Eddie.

"You know, I have never tasted a TV personality before," the Big Bad Wolf smiled with teeth as sharp as icicles, "and certainly not a chat-show host."

Chapter 8

At FIZZ TV, Sadie has come up in the world.

She now has her own office with SADIE TUFFETT – PRODUCER written on the door, and she also has her own chat show.

The viewers seem to like her. She is pretty and sometimes witty. Some of her guests can be interesting to listen to. Only last night she interviewed a Do-It-Yourself expert who has written a book called *A Thousand and One Uses for Old Tights*. She also interviewed a lady who has left a fortune in her will to a dolphin named Fred. Through a TV link-up with Florida she was also able to talk to Fred, and really, he was the star of the show.

Right now Sadie is practising her closing speech for this evening's show. Let us listen in to what she will say to perhaps eleven or twelve million viewers in their own homes:

"And that's all we have time for tonight, ladies and gentlemen. My name is Sadie Tuffett, this is FIZZ TV, do join me at the same time tomorrow for another edition of the nation's favourite chat show.

"If you would like to appear on the show please get in touch with us here at FIZZ TV. Do not apply if you are dull and boring – and DEFINITELY NO WOLVES. Thank you and … good night."

THE TIME SAILORS

Ian Whybrow

Ten-year-old Edward finds his visits to Grandad
Wilson's house a bit of a trial – especially when
Great Aunt Spud is there fussing away. She's
there today, and Grandad Wilson is being as rude
and awkward as ever – refusing to let her dust his
silver pocket watch or the fading brown photo
which Edward loves. It shows two boys –
Grandad Wilson and his friend Futter – by a river
with an oar and an old-fashioned pram. But it's
the cloth cap, floating in the air between them,
that intrigues Edward. What's it doing there?
Who does it belong to?

BEETLE AND THE BIOSPHERE

Susan Gates

Down among the wilderness of the sand dunes stand six wooden shacks, commonly known as the Ramshackles. Beetle's grandpa and Abby's grandma live there, which is how the two children come to meet. At first they seem like chalk and cheese: Beetle, fanatical player of Fantasy Adventure Games, and serious, scientific Abby, creator of the silver tent-like biosphere. But when vandals strike and the dunes come under threat, it seems as if only these two unlikely allies can save the Ramshackles!

Follow the imaginative exploits of Beetle and Abby in this exhilarating adventure story.